Walt Disney's Donald Duck

Some Ducks Have All the Luck

A GOLDEN BOOK • NEW YORK

Western Publishing Company, Inc., Racine, Wisconsin 53404

© 1987 The Walt Disney Company. All rights reserved. Printed in the U.S.A. by Western Publishing Company, Inc. No part of this book may be reproduced or copied in any form without written permission from the copyright owner. GOLDEN®, GOLDEN & DESIGN®, A GOLDEN BOOK®, and A LITTLE GOLDEN BOOK® are trademarks of Western Publishing Company, Inc. Library of Congress Catalog Card Number: 86-83072 ISBN: 0-307-01020-1   MCMXC

Donald Duck was pacing the floor.
"Uncle Donald…" said Huey.
"What's wrong?" asked Dewey.
"You're making us dizzy!" cried Louie.
"Today is Daisy's birthday," declared Donald, "and I need to get her a better present than Gladstone Gander."

"That's easy, Uncle Donald," said Huey.
"Just get Daisy a bigger, fancier present than he does," said Dewey.

"But Gladstone's so lucky, and I'm broke," Donald complained. "He'll probably buy Daisy something expensive. And besides, how can I buy something better when I don't even know what he's giving her?"

Just then Donald glanced out the window and noticed someone walking down the street.

"Gladstone Gander!" he exclaimed. "Maybe it's my lucky day after all. I'll follow him all over town until I see what he's buying for Daisy."

Gladstone Gander was worrying, too.

"I sure hope I get lucky today. I have to come up with a really great present for Daisy," he thought as he walked along.

"Ah, this must be my good luck now!" Gladstone exclaimed when he saw some money lying on the sidewalk. But it was only a one-dollar bill.

"Every little bit helps," Gladstone said with a sigh as he put the bill in his pocket.

When he started walking again, Gladstone Gander had a funny feeling. "I'm being followed," he thought.

Gladstone stopped at a jewelry store and pretended to look in the window.

He chuckled when he recognized Donald's reflection in the store window.

"I bet Donald is as worried about Daisy's present as I am," thought Gladstone. "I know how to give him a real scare!"

Gladstone Gander marched into the jewelry store and looked at some diamond bracelets. He held them up, just to make sure Donald saw.

Outside, poor Donald Duck groaned. "That must have been a thousand-dollar bill he just found! Now he's buying Daisy a diamond bracelet. Some ducks have all the luck!" Donald thought.

Gladstone's next stop was the Bonbon Boutique, which sold the most expensive chocolates in Duckburg.

Donald went into the store after Gladstone came out. He almost fainted when the clerk told him the price of one 14-Karat Chocolate Bonbon.

Donald caught up with Gladstone Gander outside the Sniff of Success Perfume Shop. Gladstone couldn't resist teasing Donald.

"Fancy meeting you here, Donald. I was just trying to decide what to give Daisy for her birthday—a diamond bracelet, a 100-Karat Chocolate Bonbon, or a bottle of Liquid Gold, 'The Perfume Too Expensive to Wear,'" said Gladstone gleefully.

Donald slunk away.

"I guess this wasn't my lucky day after all," he thought. "I never should have followed Gladstone. He has all the luck."

Gladstone Gander enjoyed his laugh. But soon he remembered that he still had no present for Daisy and only one dollar in his pocket.

"I need some good luck, and I need it now!" thought Gladstone as he hurried home.

"Hello, Mr. Gander," said the mail carrier. "I just left a special-delivery letter in your mailbox."

"Maybe I've won another contest," Gladstone thought as he tore open the envelope. He read eagerly, "You have been selected to receive dinner for two at the grand opening of Chez Swann, the swankiest restaurant in Duckburg."

Gladstone whooped. "My good luck strikes again! This is the perfect present for Daisy. Donald doesn't have a chance."

Meanwhile, Donald Duck was sadly climbing the steps of his house.

"We have a surprise for you, Uncle Donald," said Huey, Dewey, and Louie.

"I'm not interested in surprises," Donald moaned.

"But we found out what Aunt Daisy wants most for her birthday, and we got it for you," said Huey.

"The present is all wrapped up and waiting in the car," added Dewey.

"So let's go!" shouted Louie, racing for the car.

Donald and his nephews had been at Daisy's house
for a little while when a knock came at the door. It
was Gladstone Gander.

"Happy birthday, dear Daisy!" Gladstone exclaimed.
"How would you like to go to the opening night of
Chez Swann, the swankiest restaurant in Duckburg?"

"I'd love to, Gladstone," Daisy replied. "But I simply can't leave my darling kitty that Donald gave me," she added, cuddling the tiny kitten until it purred and purred and purrrrred.

"I have an idea! Why don't you and Donald have my birthday dinner together? You can sing 'Happy Birthday' to me," Daisy said, showing them both to the door.

Donald Duck had a great time at Chez Swann. He
lifted his glass and toasted, "To Daisy and her kitty!"
"To Daisy," Gladstone Gander agreed. Then he
grumbled, "Some ducks have all the luck."